Chapter 1

A young chocolate African American drives a huge cock over her tender lips, takes off her lace panties and sniffs them greedily, the girl obviously likes it. She tries to wrap her mouth around his penis, but fails to tame it. They kiss passionately. A lean African American caresses her swollen nipples with his tongue, descends lower and lower ... Her pussy becomes wet and obscenely wet. He continues to caress her clitoris with his tongue, she moans, experiencing pleasant pleasure. The young stallion spreads her legs and is ready to enter her inflamed bosom.

What?! Are you out of your mind?! I will not do it! Diana says.

Of course, the choice is always yours. The pornographer answers. Nobody is going to force you. But in all other cases, I can't give you money.

You are clearly overreacting! Am I supposed to fuck with them?

Of course. The pornographer taunts. You're not going to play peepers with them. Here is another scenario, here almost everything is the same.

Brazen bastard! It turns out she is again sucking an African American's cock like a caramel lollipop. He swallows it deeper and deeper ... He pulls off her light lace panties, sniffs them greedily and throws them aside. She lies on her back and spreads her legs, he tickles her vagina with his huge hot rod. She is inflamed to the limit and wants him to enter her. But the African American does not dare to join the fight, he greedily drives a red-hot penis between her compressed breasts and cums dirty on her face. A second African American appears, he festively uncorks a bottle of champagne, drinks himself and gives the heroine a taste, the thick foam of champagne resembles the sperm that the first brother in arms released. The second African American caresses her breasts with kisses and is completely naked, taking off his clothes. Diana begins to take turns sucking their cocks ... Then they all lie down on the bed together and animal caresses begin here as if she is a real tigress in the mating season. Dark males passionately lick her body. She squeezes into a fist, then a member of one, then the second, and plays with their penises like an insatiable cat. Then Diana tickles their soft scrotums with her tongue, and then wraps her lips around them. One holds her by the hair and thereby intercepts the initiative, because he has not yet released a sticky web into her mouth. A moment ... And Diana's mouth is filled with tart sticky ligature. She swallows it like a raw chicken egg and dissolves in sweet bliss, wrapping herself in a bed blanket.

Are you taking me for a whore?! Diana is outraged. Did it ever occur to you that I have honor and dignity?!

I repeat again. The Pornographer says firmly. No one is going to make a slave out of you. Everything is only voluntary ... And if you don’t like something, go to the bank and take a loan.

You know that with my official salary, I can only borrow a TV. I ask for a loan from you, I really need this money.

Who doesn't need them? Everyone needs money.

I give you my word, I will repay the debt.

Your words to me to one place ... As you can see, I work in the erotic business, not in a credit institution.

You know. Diana sobs. If I don't find money for my mother's treatment, she will die! I will give, I will work, but only in a different way. I'm ready for anything but this...

Are you talking about everything? It turns out that not everything ... The Pornographer grins.

I used to be your girlfriend. First love... We kissed at school, remember? Also, you said...

Come on, I'm not interested in your old memories. We were young and naive. What was, is gone. Moreover, the old feelings will never be the same. Why all this graduation party?

The pornographer is distracted by the smartphone screen and with a smug grin writes a message to someone for a long time.

I will only do this for my sick mother. After a long pause, Diana whispers. If I don't find the money for the operation, she will die.

Now that's another conversation. Exactly thirteen days you will star in my new film. Throughout this time, you will be mine, from head to toe. I will do with you what I see fit, but in return you will receive a huge amount of money. I think the game is worth the candle, especially when it comes to the health of your mother.

Damn you! Diana breaks down. I hate you! It's better to die in complete poverty than to deal with a bastard like you!

So do good to people after that. The Pornographer says calmly. You can't earn that much in a year working at your regular job. And here it’s only thirteen days… Especially at school, it seems you went to a theater group? So here we will have almost the same thing, only for adults. And I pay for it as an adult. Business is business.

I accept your terms. Diana speaks through tears. I will play this part.

Chapter 2

The house shone with decoration, everything was ready for the celebration. They decided to celebrate in a narrow family circle. Moreover, the occasion was delicate, the engagement of the youngest daughter. This event was decided to coincide with my mother's birthday. Therefore, the guest list consisted only of the closest people. Birthday mother, daughter with the groom and her older sister.

Karina is late as usual! Bride Diana called out from the kitchen.

Yes, Karinka is always like that. Mom confirmed. A very unpunctual person.

Cut onion into salad?

Today it's better not to, enough

tears from us. Let now there will be a holiday on our street!

Oh yes! I completely forgot ... Since you are still in such a good mood, I have to tell you the most unpleasant news. I quit my job…

Mom dropped the salad bowl from her hands, the crystal bowl shattered, and a hundred small fragments sparkled like frozen ice crystals in the sun.

How are we going to live now? Mom got worried.

And how did we live before that, when I studied at the institute? Diana swept her former well-being into the scoop.

Mom, dejectedly thoughtful and did not know how to answer this question correctly, the experience was interrupted by the doorbell.

Mom, can you help me replace it? The unemployed daughter exclaimed and rushed to open the door.

Opening the door, Diana sees a drunken groom named Ephraim on the threshold. Clutching a battered bouquet of flowers in one hand, the groom is trying to uncork a small check of vodka with the other hand.

I hope I'm not too late? Ephraim asks with concern.

No, you're even early.

Good! Hello mummy! Excuse me, can I use a little to dilate blood vessels?

It is possible, but not necessary. Mom replies sharply. Let's sit down at the table and have a drink. More success.

The owner of the bar. Ephraim agrees and whispers in Diana's ear. Listen, I've mortgaged our future apartment here on account of the debt. Be a friend, give me a hundred dollars before payday?

Then we'll discuss, not in front of

my mother. Diana hisses and steps on Ephraim's foot.

What are you whispering? Mom is worried. You know the saying, more than two speak aloud?

Mom, Karina texted me saying she'll be here in an hour. Diana lied and squinted angrily at Ephraim.

I knew that she would be late again, I didn't spank her enough in my childhood. Mom complains and flops down in a chair from fatigue.

Can you sit down then? Ephraim revives. Why pull it?!

Ephraim pours champagne into glasses, at this moment the elder sister Karina appears. Angrily throwing the keys on the bedside table, Karina starts to make a fuss.

Ah… Are you already here celebrating without me?! Karina explodes. I live in a rented apartment, and here you are drinking champagne! Well settled down.

Girls, let's not fight. Innocent Ephraim breaks in.

Shut up! All three women besiege him with one voice.

I've been talking for a long time. The sister continues. Let's change this apartment!

Yep, let's change! The mother explodes. And where will I live?

We'll buy you a room in a communal flat. The sister answers. Or we can put you in a nursing home. There is nothing terrible in this ...

Diana tries to calm her psychotic sister, but Karina loses control and pours dirty insults on her own mother. The mother grabs her heart and loses consciousness. Diana, in a panic, calls an ambulance team, which diagnoses a stroke.

***

Diana sat in the emergency room until morning. Waiting for the doctor, she heard disappointing facts.

The situation is deplorable. The doctor said dryly. hemorrhagic stroke. In the near future, paralysis of the limbs is possible.

What to do? Diana asked, flushing.

What to do... What to do... The doctor began to fuss. It is being treated, that's what to do .... But such treatment, you understand, is paid. If there are financial opportunities, there are chances. But no, it's all the will of God ...

How much money is needed?

The doctor wrote the sum with six zeros on a piece of paper. And cynically added:

Don't worry, it's in rubles.

Diana realized this was the end. She is unlikely to be able to get such a huge amount, especially in the near future. Leaving the hospital door, she called Ephraim. She wanted to find in him a soul mate, peace, support, consolation ... But she heard: “You know, you are a good girl. But my soul does not lie. Nothing will work for us." After an unpleasant conversation with Ephraim, Diana immediately receives a WhatsApp notification from her sister. By clicking on the round green icon, opening the message, she sees a joint photo of Karina and Ephraim, and below the caption: "My new boyfriend and we are going to St. Petersburg together for the weekend." Dropping the phone from her hands, Diana covered her face with her hands and began to cry.

Karina is an old whore! Didn't you beat my guys at school?! And now you can't calm down? It was insulting and bitter in my soul ... This is her own sister! And here it is! Betrayal is felt many times more acutely if it comes from people close to you. It's like a stab in the back, from those who have to lend a shoulder in difficult times.

Staggering in a haze of despair through the deserted city streets, Diana sees the sparkling signboard of the alcobar and decides to stop by. It won't get worse anyway... How much worse? What else is so terrible that can happen to her? Will she be forced to act in porn where she is fucked by muscular blacks? This is definitely too much, she doesn't need such a gift from fate. She has already been fucked enough by her own sister, as well as her former fiancé Ephraim. So fucked that sperm is now pouring from all ears.

Having entered the bar and thought a little, where is it better for her to sit at the bar or at the table? Diana sees her first school love ... He sits alone at the table and stares intently in her direction. She remembered those sad blue eyes shining with sadness. His first kisses, caresses, hugs. School evening, when he walked her home and this sluggish attempt to have sex for the first time in the stairwell. Suddenly, something cut in my chest, and my soul became so disgusting and vile, as if a bad tooth had been pulled out without anesthesia. Still, after all, she was betrayed again! They spat in the soul and thoroughly wiped their feet, threw them out. The ugly duckling Diana almost believed that there is true love and sincere feelings in life. But faith burst like a balloon. She truly gave herself to him, and in return received a treacherous stab in the back.

She was in pain, but she endured and, like a real actress, masterfully coped with the role. After intercourse, he asked her for one nude photo service. Diana at first answered with a harsh refusal, but then she still succumbed to persuasion and agreed. Moreover, it was only about one photograph ... He photographed her body, capturing all the delights of young beauty in the image. He said that he would keep this photo to the very heart, remembering each time about their true love. But he lied, after a few days, this photo became the property of the entire school and went from hand to hand like a reusable condom. It turned out that he had bet with his classmate that he could spin even such a shy mess for an erotic picture. They laughed at Diana, humiliated her, called her a prostitute, and simply hated her, because she truly sincerely fell in love and gave herself completely without a trace. After this incident, he received the nickname Pornographer, and she remained a gullible victim of male deceptions. Years later, they met again at a bar.

What the hell is he handsome! Time has not spoiled it, but on the contrary, like good wine, it has only made it better. Blond hair, a luxurious suit, a toned figure and a charming look that has been carefully studying her for several minutes. She hasn't seen Pornographer since high school (he seems to have been relegated). However, she heard a lot about him from mutual acquaintances. It was from them that she learned that he took place in business and leads a mysterious lifestyle. In a word, a successful millionaire is a handsome man of marriageable age. It is about such specimens that almost all women dream of, dreaming of getting such a thoroughbred individual as a legal husband.

***

He got up from the table and walked towards the bar.

Thank God I didn't know. Diana breathed out.

But he dreamed about her almost every week. Even while having sex with Ephraim, she sometimes imagined that she was having sex with a Pornographer. Oh, if her erotic fantasies turned into reality... She stands doggystyle and dripping juice like a dirty bitch, Pornographer kneels from behind and smoothly enters her. He fucks her doggystyle, and she moans, experiencing one of the strongest pleasures on earth. His hot, bloodshot cock throbs deeper and deeper, so that she feels a pleasant pain as well, making light moaning sounds. His confident movements leave her no choice, and she is forced to scream: “Fuck me! Yes, fuck! Take me to exhaustion! I'm yours! I'm yours! Oh my God! How good! How good I am!" The pornographer slaps her buttocks with his palm and wraps her hair around his fist with the other hand. Her juicy, ripe ass is obscenely red, but Diana is turned on by rough spanking. She wants more, and more. She squeals and groans after every blow from the Pornographer. But these are only flowers ... The pornographer puts the thumb of his left hand into her anus and gently stimulates the anus. Diana feels a little discomfort, but then a pleasant pain follows, her body shudders in spasms, the Pornographer wraps her hair around her fist even tighter. He feels like a god and ruler of her body, any of his movements causes convulsions of mini orgasms in her, which is why she wants the Pornographer even more. Continuing to kneel and fucking Diana doggystyle, he aggressively squeezes her breasts and speeds up her movements. Then the Pornographer pulls out his wet cock, which is soaked in the nectar of Diane's vagina. He drives his wet cock along the partner's labia, as if thinking at that moment whether to cum in her or not? Diana spreads her legs, making it clear that her body craves his sperm, she wants him to penetrate her to the end. She abruptly grabs the Pornographer's legs and puts him on the shoulder blades, sitting on his wet and hot cock. With the feeling of a wild cowgirl, strong movements, she saddles a heated stallion and receives violent ejaculation as a reward ... How sweet her erotic fantasies are! But these are just fantasies… Diana opens her eyes and a half-drunk Yefrem lies on her, exuding a pungent smell of fumes. Ephraim is tormented by shortness of breath, he groans and after a short silence, says: “I have finished ... I hope you too?”. Diana, without saying anything, closes her eyes, lying that she is also satisfied. Although in fact she did not feel almost anything, except for the fetid fumes of her partner. What a cool and sexy

Pornographer! He is the true ideal man of her dreams. But where is she before him? He is probably married, or certainly not vegetating alone. In any case, he hardly sits and waits for the same Diana with whom he once had a small school affair, because he was her first man, and not vice versa. Therefore, it makes no sense to approach him, for sure he will not even recognize her. And if he finds out, what will she tell him? I am an unemployed loser, my mother is in the hospital with a stroke ... In general, a marriageable dowry. Usually, men stay away from such persons and run from such "brides" like from fire. It's better to just go unnoticed and continue to be in dreams, constantly thinking about the unattainable image of an ideal man.

Diana, is that you? The Pornographer asks, holding two glasses of wine in his hand.

Oh gods! Oh gods! So calm, how do I look?! I must have run out of mascara ... If only not to go crazy with fear.

Ahh .... Excuse me, do we know each other?

What are you?! Remember at school? We've met before... Then, stuttering, the Pornographer pauses.

Oh, yes ... Diana smiles feignedly. I remember something.

May I serve you? The pornographer holds out a glass of wine. My table is in the corner. Are you in a hurry? Maybe we can have dinner together.

Diana, blushing, is silent.

What's wrong, are you married?

Yes. Oh, that is no. Almost, not quite. In short, I am not married.

And then I started to worry.

Oh... No, what are you...

I hope you do not carry on the image of an old maid and accept my invitation?

Diana, with a trembling hand, wants to take a glass of wine from the Pornographer, but accidentally drops it and the glass shatters. Diana, in a panic, wants to quickly pick up the pieces, but her hands are trembling and she cuts her finger.

Leave, leave! A young student waitress screams. I'll take it all away now.

Yes, please help us. Pornographer says.

Oh, it's you. The waitress is embarrassed. And I've been waiting for your call. You probably wrote down my number incorrectly? Can we meet after work today?

Feeling superfluous and burning with shame, Diana wraps her finger in a napkin and runs to the toilet.

***

Sitting on the toilet, Diana cries.

She is so lousy at heart that she wants to hang herself. It's always like this! Karina has been beating her boyfriends since school. First she took the Pornographer away, and now she has gone to St. Petersburg with her future fiancé Ephraim. Karina has always lived beyond her means and always wanted more than she has ... And poor Diana is again on the sidelines of fate. An evil curse is definitely hanging on her, she is like a leper and it is clear she will never marry, at least not in this life. Wiping tears with a bloody napkin. Diana caught herself thinking that she had nowhere to get money for treatment for her mother. Karina, as usual, doesn't care about anything, especially the health of her own mother. She had already made it clear long ago that her mother was not interested in her at all, and she only needed her apartment. Diana began to cry again, suddenly the toilet door opened and she saw the Pornographer in front of her.

Chapter 3

Are you okay? He asks. How's the finger?

Fine. Just tingles a little...

Well, it's not scary. Before the wedding must pass. Moreover, this is not a finger for wearing a wedding ring.

Are you joking like that? Diana asked dumbfounded. This is clearly not funny...

No, this is how I express my love.

In love? To whom me? Diana was confused.

Admit it, you thought about me, didn't you? Seriously asked the Pornographer, unzipped his fly and took out an elastic penis.

A little embarrassed, Diana closed her eyes and timidly began to stroke the member of the Pornographer, swollen with excitement. Then she timidly swallows the red head and begins to caress it with her mouth. Swallowing the member of the Pornographer deeper and deeper, almost to the very testicles, he awkwardly slips out of her mouth, then she begins to caress the penis with her hands, gently tugging and squeezing it in her fist. Alternating actions in such a way as to give the Pornographer maximum pleasure. She also caresses his penis with her lips and tongue, the Pornographer relaxes her hair, controlling the movements of her head. The insatiable Pornographer squeezes her head with his palms and begins to make active movements with his pelvis, introducing his cock at insane speed into Dianin's mouth. Diana has accepted the terms of the game and moves her head in time with the movements of the Pornographer.

She clearly likes his cruelty. He grabbed her by the throat with one hand and cums in her mouth. After swallowing his pale cloudy sperm, Diana opened her eyes again and is ready to taste the forbidden nectar again. But the Pornographer, with a cynical movement of his hand, zipped up his fly and threw his business card into her lap. With a wink in farewell, he opened the door and left, leaving behind a pleasant aftertaste.

***

Coming out of the toilet to the bar, Diana only now realized that she had sat in the booth almost until morning. Dawn broke through the windows. Oral sex with Pornographer did not let her go so much that she forgot about everything in the world.

Girl, what are you doing here? An old cleaner calls out to her.

Yes, I am ... I just got lost

here. Diana lied. Where can you drink water here?

Yep, water! The cleaner was outraged. Would you like some more gin and tonic?

No thanks, that's overkill. Did not understand the sarcasm of the cleaning lady Diana. You can just plain water without gas.

Yep, no gas! The cleaning lady blew up. Well, get the hell out of here you filthy slut! Before I called the police… God, what kind of place are they thinking of here?! There used to be a canteen here, how nice! No, they should have made a bar with these whores. Now they roam here day and night, they don’t let them work quietly.

Diana rushed out of the bar, quietly muttering through her teeth: "The bitch herself is old."

But apparently the cleaning lady was all right with her hearing, and she shouted after her: “Let's scratch the seven-breasted larva from here!”. After leaving the ill-fated bar, Diana found that she had no cash at all. Public transport is still not running, the phone is dead and there are no taxis nearby. There is only one way out in such a situation, to go on foot.

Walking along the side of the road, drivers honked every now and then, inviting Diana to spend time together. But Diana, not paying any attention to them, proudly walked forward, and did not even think about leaving them her phone number. Suddenly Diana was called out by a woman's voice from a nearby car.

Dianka! Are you?!

Diana turned around.

The woman's face seemed familiar to her, but she could not remember where she had seen him.

Excuse me, do we know each other? Diana asked.

Well you give a girlfriend! Didn't you know?

Diana shook her head negatively.

Sorry no…

Have I really changed that much? Well remember! Eighth grade, they sat together at the same desk ...

Zhanka! Diana exclaimed. Wow!

Get in, I'll take you! And then move the horses until you reach!

While driving, the friends started talking, and Zhanna told Diana about her personal life. She is divorced, there is no one on the personal front, she recently broke up with a mutual friend from school. With whom would you think? With the Pornographer!

Guess you didn't even call me back! Goat! Zhanna complained to her friend.

Yeah… Diana sighed reproachfully.

And how are you personally? Is there anyone?

So far I'm only sucking on the handle of the frying pan. Diana scoffed.

At least you have something to suck on. Jeanne summed up enviously and drove her school friend home.

Do you still live there?

Yep, right there. Diana confirmed.

Looks like they've almost arrived. Are you sure you don't want to go poop?

I'm sorry Zhannochka, but I don't have the strength anymore. Diana politely refused.

As you know ... And that is, there is one bar here. By the way, I picked you up near him. Such a cool place…

No, then I don't want to. Diana interrupted. Stop here please. It's not far, I'll walk.

No problem. You call, do not disappear, if that.

Deal! Diana slammed the door and slowly walked towards the house.

Although, to be honest, I didn't want to go home at all. Diana sat down on a bench in the courtyard near her house and felt homesick. A middle-aged man with two children came out of the entrance. On the left is a boy and on the right is a girl. "Apparently leading them to kindergarten, thought Diana. But she is still not married and nothing good looms on the horizon. Life is terribly unfair! Sick mother, lack of money, lack of work…". Suddenly, Diana noticed that a light was on in the windows of her apartment. Who could it be? Diana felt uncomfortable and terrified that some strangers might be in her apartment. With fear, having risen to her floor and opening the front door, Diana heard rustling.

***

Slowly entering the room where the strange sounds were coming from,

Diana was trembling with fear. She saw an open closet. A white dove flew out of the closet, made several circles around the room, frighteningly flapping its wings, the dove knocked down several crystal vases and flew out through the open window, disappearing in an unknown direction. Being in a state of shock, Diana looked around every corner of the apartment and found with reassurance that there was no one, lay down on the sofa and fell asleep.

Diana, what are you doing? Did your daughter fall asleep?

Someone stroked Diana on the back. Diana opened her eyes and saw her mother.

Mom, why aren't you in the hospital?

So they released me today. The doctor said there was no more reason to keep me there.

How is that not a reason?

He says, since there is no money, then there is nothing to occupy a place. He says that it makes no sense to lie here anyway, since there is no money for treatment. And you can just lie on the bed and at home.

Diana began to cry, her mother hugged her and kindly began to calm her upset daughter.

Mom, do you remember when I was in school and was in the hospital with gastritis? Did you pass the potato pies to me through the nurse?

Mother solicitously confirmed.

Of course I remember.

Do you also remember, when I wanted to steal a book from the school library, you made such a scandal and made me return the book.

And I remember that too. The mother confirmed again.

Mother hugged Diana tightly and kissed her on the forehead. Diana lay down on her side with her hands under her head, closed her eyes and remembered her childhood. A young mother prepares breakfast for her and helps her get ready for school by tying two beautiful bows on her head.

Mom, this is old fashioned! Diana snaps.

The most beautiful and fashionable girl, Dianochka. The mother does not agree.

Diana opened her eyes and found that while she was sleeping someone had covered her with a warm checkered blanket. Beloved mother, she always takes care of me, how I love you! But suddenly there was a knock at the door.

Mom! The doorbell is ringing!

There was no answer.

Mom! Where are you?! Diana screamed again.

The call got louder. Frightened, Diana to the peephole and without looking opened the door. Sister Karina and former fiancé Ephraim stood on the threshold.

Chapter 4

Where is mom? Diana asked shocked.

Where? Karina answered cynically. She died. We will be buried tomorrow.

How did she die? Diana couldn't believe her ears.

How everyone dies ... So she died.

The earth rest in peace to her. Ephraim added.

By the way, what are you doing in my apartment? Karina asked. Come on, get out of here!

Why is she yours? Diana asked.

The will must be read... Ephraim, throw her out of here.

Karish, my leg hurts, I sprained it yesterday... And I saw beer in the fridge, can I have one sip?

Not a man, but a rag! It's disgusting to even wipe your feet on you! As usual, you have to do everything yourself! Karina said sharply and clung to Diana with a fierce grip of a predator.

Arriving in a state of shock, Diana grabbed scissors from the table and plunged them into her sister's throat. Immediately blood gushed out, and the white tablecloth turned crimson in an instant. Staggering aside, Diana covered her face with her hands and wept hysterically. Sobbing madly, horrified and not believing that she was able to commit murder.

Diana, what have you done? The drunk Ephraim asked in fright and ran away to call the police.

***

Something broke, and then rustled its wings ... Diana opened her eyes and saw the same dove, which she had already driven out of the apartment. Turning her head to the right, she saw another broken vase and a dove flying around the room. Diana grabbed a pillow and with the words: “Well, hold on! Flying Animal! Kicked the uninvited guest away. Sitting on the sofa and hugging the pillow, she whispered aloud in puzzlement: “Was it really a dream?” Diana looked at the scissors lying on the table and, making sure that there was not a drop of blood on them, she calmed down. After removing the fragments and deciding to take a shower, naked Diana stood under the stream of water. Warm water gently caressed her body and washed away all the dirt of the previous night. After a relaxing shower, Diana brewed strong coffee and rummaged through her purse for a long time, finally found the Pornographer's business card. Long thinking, call or not? Diana nervously weighed all the arguments, pros and cons. But the total lack of money and the hopelessness of the situation, all these depressing circumstances, forced me to call the Pornographer.

***

Calling and writing down the detailed address, Diana called a taxi. The chatty taxi driver, realizing that the interlocutor was not making contact, turned on the chanson at full volume and stared lazily at the road, until the end of the trip he did not say a word. “God, where did he take me?”, thought Diana. Some kind of slums, hangars and warehouses, a gloomy industrial area. On the spot, everything turned out to be much gloomier. The old shabby building she was supposed to enter did not inspire anything good. The iron front door creaked like something out of a horror movie, and Diana entered the

Pornographer's lair.

Inside the building were film sets with video cameras everywhere. Diana felt uncomfortable in an unfamiliar place, but after finding the Pornographer's office, she became a little calmer.

Come on in and have a seat. The pornographer pointed to a chair.

Diana sat silently.

I understand you're a little puzzled. The pornographer smiled. But it's very cheap here. That's why we chose this place. Cheap and cheerful.

Yeah, you've always had good taste...

Tastes could not be discussed. Interrupted
Pornographer. Let's get straight to the point. Didn't you come here to chat?

After carefully listening to the story of the mother's illness and delicately specifying the required amount, the Pornographer was silent for several minutes, and then said: "Of course, I will give you money, but there is one caveat ...".

Nuance? What's the nuance? Diana sensed a trick.

Will you star in my new film? I hope you noticed that there are film sets here?

Wait, what movie?

The entire filming process took only thirteen days.

But I'm not an actress, am I?

Believe me, your talent will be quite enough. Here's the script, take a look. The pornographer held out a small stack of papers.

***

I accept your terms. Diana speaks through tears. I will play this part.

Good! The pornographer clapped his hands. Now we will sign the contract. Let me read you the terms.

You will receive the designated

amount of money. In return, you will take part in the filming of my new porn film as the main actress. Filming will take place over thirteen days. Now let's go through the points.

Item number 1. Unquestioningly comply with the requirements of the director for all thirteen days.

Item number 2. Everything that will happen to you on the set is already approved by you in advance. Therefore, not subject to objection.

Item number 3. Your main task is to simulate an orgasm.

Item number 4. Bodily injuries received during the filming are related to the costs of the profession and are not paid additionally.

Item number 5. You must not leave this building.

Item number 6. You must also provide a certificate of absence of sexually transmitted diseases.

Item number 7. It is your

responsibility to maintain personal hygiene on a daily basis.

Item number 8. All copyrights on videos with your participation belong to the film studio.

Item number 9. It is forbidden to use mobile phones and the Internet without prior approval.

Item number 10. If at least one of the clauses of this contract is violated by you. Then the transferred money will be immediately frozen, and the contract will be canceled.

When he finished reading the list of requirements, the Pornographer handed Diana a contract and a fountain pen. After reading the conditions again more carefully, Diana began to doubt.

And what is this camera in the corner under the ceiling? she asked. Are we being filmed now?

What camera? The pornographer hesitated. Oh, this one... Don't worry, it's just a legal formality. The recording is for personal use only.

I don't want her filming me now. Including for personal use. Diana put her fountain pen aside.

Filming is being done so that there is a confirming video that you are in sound memory and in a sober mind, voluntarily sign a contract. There is no other subtext here, I assure you.

Diana was puzzled.

The final decision is of course yours. But poor mother, how is she now in the hospital?

Wiping her tears with a napkin, Diana grabbed a fountain pen and nervously signed. Legally agreeing with the voiced requirements. Making sure that the signature is in the right place, smiling devilishly, Pornographer delivered a verdict: "Now your body is mine."

Only for thirteen days. Diana said proudly.

You are now my slave, even if only for thirteen days. Therefore, we will not start filming right now!

Like now?! I'm not ready!

A contract is a contract. There is no way back.

I need to say goodbye to my mom. I won't be here for almost two weeks. Let me go... Just one day.

Okay, you can take a paid day off tomorrow... Now get to work! Two African Americans are already waiting for you.

Chapter 5

Diana walked down the deserted street and regretted her act. Why did she agree? You should never make hasty decisions before hitting rock bottom. It is necessary to use all the options so that, like a frog from a parable, which landed in a jar of milk, without falling into despair, vigorously floundering with its paws, turned it into butter. Inspired Diana, bouncing along the street and planning to return to her former job, she sincerely believed that she would be taken back, then she would be able to break the contract with the Pornographer and take a loan for the treatment of her mother.

But fate turned out to be much tougher, the former boss listened carefully to her request, but shook his head negatively, saying: “No, no one is waiting for you here ... Go away when you leave.” Diana ran out of his office in tears. Walking quickly along the desks where former colleagues were sitting, it seemed to Diana that she saw herself and the Pornographer on one of the monitors. In the video, she nervously signed the contract, and the Pornographer smiled cynically.

It can be seen that my roof is already going completely, all my thoughts are mixed up. Diana thought aloud. You need to see a doctor urgently! Visit Mom...

A visit to the hospital did not bring anything good, but only exacerbated the picture of a gloomy day. Mom got worse, she was lying unconscious under drips. There were a lot of transparent plastic tubes sticking out of it ... Fortunately, there was still time to correct the situation, the doctor firmly assured that if the money was within two weeks, then mom could still be roused from bed.

What if I don't get the money? Diana asked.

If you don't get it... The doctor thought. Then we will still lift her out of bed, only into the coffin.

God, why do I need all this?! Diana asked herself in despair. Sell your body to save your old mother. Maybe it's her fate, to die of a stroke? And here I am fussing, running around, looking for money ... Why ?! Extra care and hassle. If my mother dies now, part of the apartment will go to me. I can then buy one with that money. And what then is the meaning of these fuckers visiting the Pornographer? Let him die... No! I cannot do otherwise. I will play this role to the end, even if I sink to the bottom.

***

Returning to the abode of the Pornographer, Diana noticed the absence of video cameras. The pavilion was empty.

Hey! Diana screamed loudly. Is there anyone?!

I'm here. A male voice answered.

Diana shuddered and turned towards the voice. She saw the Pornographer. Losing for a moment the power of speech, Diana dazedly examined him from head to toe. The pornographer was dressed the way he dressed at school. Wrinkled denim suit, bright T-shirt and blue sneakers with white stripes.

Anyone have high school memories? The pornographer asked sarcastically.

No, I'm just looking. Diana lied in a trembling voice.

Look good.

As you say. Diana smiled.

There is a dressing room right down the hallway. There is a chest in the dressing room, a suit in the chest. Put it on and come back here, I'll be waiting for you.

Diana was thoughtfully silent.

Hey! Ay! Do you understand?! The Pornographer asked angrily.

Yes. Diana perked up. Certainly. What can be incomprehensible here? A chest on a tree, a tree on an island, an egg in a chest, a needle in an egg.

The pornographer laughed out loud ... In the locker room, Diana really found a chest, and in the chest there was an erotic costume and a whip. Having picked up such an accessory for love pleasures for the first time, Diana turned it over in her hands, and then tried several times to hit her ass with it.

Ay! Hurt! Diana yelled and put the whip aside.

Then she pulled on her latex gear, pulling all the laces and straps tight. Carefully studying her new image, looking at herself in the mirror, Diana did not like that black latex tightly fits the figure and indecently emphasizes all the eroticism of the appetizing body. "What vulgarity!" thought Diana. Her breasts protruded from a deep cleavage, and sharp nipples stuck out, hinting at excessive arousal. In the corner, she noticed high-heeled shoes and tried them on too. Looking again at herself in all her glory in the mirror, Diana realized that now she was just a dirty whore, a sex toy! A doll made of latex and leather, which can be manipulated and pulled by the strings at any order of the Pornographer. Tears came to Diana's eyes again, she opened the locker to get paper napkins and saw a suit similar to Harley Quinn.

***

Having made a bright make-up, Diana left the dressing room in the form of Harley Quinn. Instead of a baseball bat, she was clutching a huge dildo in her hands. Returning to the hall, from where the Pornographer sent her to change clothes, Diana saw him sitting with his back to her. The pacified Pornographer relaxed drinking tea and was unaware of the danger behind him. Diana tightened her grip on the dildo and slowly crept up to the Pornographer with slow steps. From the speakers played light relaxing music with the singing of birds, the Pornographer took a small porcelain teapot from the table and poured himself more tea into a cup. Taking a bite of some oatmeal cookies, he took a small sip, closed his eyes, trying to completely immerse himself in listening to music. Diana was already a few steps away from him, clutching the dildo like a baseball bat. Yet here she is, and she will hit him on the head with a huge and heavy semblance of a penis! Making a swing, she closed her eyes in fear and struck.

***

As soon as Diana closed her eyes, Pornographer abruptly jumped up from his seat, hitting the back of the chair.

Completely freaked out?! Stupid! The Pornographer in the image of the Joker shouted.

Diana dropped the heavy phallus from her hands and stared at the made-up Pornographer. The pallor of his face and bloody smile matched his sequined suit. The pornographer kicked the artificial phallus. The blow sent the phallus flying to the side.

I'm asking you, are you crazy? Boiling, yelled Pornographer.

Diana stood still and did not answer.

On your knees, creature! The Pornographer ordered furiously.

Diana continued not to respond to his cries.

Do you want me to break the contract and leave you without money?!

The pornographer pressed on the sore spot. Diana immediately came out of the trance, remembered her dying mother and dutifully carried out the order of the Pornographer.

So it's better, scum ... Now get up

with cancer and lift your skirt.

Diana complied with this request, she was on all fours in the middle of the room. It was the strangest thing for her to experience such depraved thoughts, but in this second she most of all wanted the Pornographer to fuck her! Fucked hard like a dirty slut from low-class porn. So that she moaned from unbearable pain, and sperm flowed down her lips.

Fuck me. Diana whispered, continuing to stand with her bare bottom on all fours.

And as if reading minds, Pornographer entered her.

Chapter 6

How did he know about Harley Quinn? Diana thought to herself.

But the Pornographer was already fucking her from behind, slapping her hot ass with his palm. And she forgot about everything in the world, sweetly enjoying anal sex. The pornographer turned out to be a real stallion, never slowing down for a second, he fucked Diana like it was the last sex of his life. Standing on all fours at Diana, her back numb, and she sank onto her stomach. At that moment, Pornographer got out of her, took Diana by the hands, put them behind her back and snapped the handcuffs. Diana sensed something was wrong ... Her intuition did not deceive her, at that very moment she felt a biting lash on her buttocks. Shouting nervously and receiving another portion of blows, Diana moaned timidly, not understanding herself whether she was moaning from pain or from bliss. When there was no living space left on the red buttocks, the Pornographer began to whip her on the back. Trembling all over, Diana convulsed, biting her lips until they bled, unable to get out of the hellish trap. She did not suspect that they were still flowers. The pornographer took the dildo with which they were going to stun him. Activating the mechanism, he inserted the vibrating rod into Diana's vagina. She experiences a cosmic orgasm, it seems to her that she is about to die from an aortic rupture, but a third partner appears, a certain girl in a red tight dress. The girl hands the Pornographer a pile of some documents and saves Diana by removing her vibrating penis.

All in bruises and abrasions, Diana lay on her side. She was exhausted and energetically devastated. From somewhere on the side, a projector lit up and Diana saw an image on the wall that she had not seen for more than ten years. A slide was inserted into the projector with only one photograph of eighteen-year-old schoolgirl Diana in the nude.

Chronic repeater Pornographer made this photo on a bet. He made a bet with a friend that he could spin the gray mouse Diana into a nude shot. And a week later, he presented everyone with evidence of his feat, spreading a naked photo of Diana throughout the school. After this incident, the handsome from the senior classes was nicknamed the Pornographer, and the whole school laughed at Diana.

Old shabby entrance, Pornographer kisses her on the lips. For Diana, this is the first kiss, the Pornographer puts his hands under her sweater... But at that moment, a dog barks from behind! An old neighbor returns from an evening walk with her pet. The pornographer pushes Diana away, quickly zips up his fly and runs down the stairs. Hearing the indignation of the old woman.

Damn perverts! Found a place!

And what are you worth, Dianka, are you shedding tears? I'll tell my mother tomorrow...

The second date went better. They met at the apartment of a friend of the Pornographer. Left alone in the room, Diana could not stand the pressure and caresses, and completely surrendered herself, trusting the Pornographer. At the end of their meeting, he asked her for one favor, to take a photo for memory. Allegedly, it will always remind him of the priceless moments that they spent together. The photo must be nude. Not noticing the trick, Diana agreed, and the Pornographer pressed the button on the Polaroid camera. Subsequently, the whole school found out about this photo ... But even when this happened, Diana, in love, believed in the innocence of the Pornographer and suggested that he run away to another city, start everything from scratch. "We will get a job as waiters! And then we'll get married ... " she said. But such romance turned out to be alien to the Pornographer and at first he simply moved away from Diana, and then completely began to ignore her, finally breaking off the relationship.

Seeing her image in the nude and remembering the vile stories from school life, Diana gradually fell into a dream, no longer feeling the pain from the blows received.

***

Diana woke up from unbearable pain, the cut skin tingled unpleasantly, and fresh scratches and abrasions burned her body. There was not a single living place left on the reddened back, where the dried blood could be seen. Diana was unable to get up and was moaning in pain lying on the floor, until the Pornographer paid attention to her.

Why are you my beauty?! He screamed in panic. So close to blood poisoning.

Diana just groaned in response to something indistinct ...

Vika! Victoria! The Pornographer screamed again.

At the call of the Pornographer, the same girl appeared in the hall, dressed in an elegant red dress, she held a jar of cream in her hands.

Nothing, nothing ... Vika said to the exhausted Diana, lubricating the affected areas of her body with cream. I have a medical background. Studied several nursing courses.

The pornographer at that moment stood behind a tripod with a video camera and pressed the record button.

Diana wanted to thank her savior, and she kissed Vika on the lips. Vika reciprocated, their tongues intertwined in mutual and quivering tickling. Diana caressed Victoria's body, stroking her breasts, thighs and buttocks. Vika rubbed her vagina on Diana's knee, feeling passionate satisfaction. Naked Diana pulled her dress up and took off Victoria's panties. Then she easily pulled off the strap from her dress and squeezed her nipple with her lips, playfully caressing the tip of the nipple with a vicious tongue. Vika stroked Diana's hair, squeezing her chest with her palm. Diana decided to go down, deciding to linger a little on the hollow of the navel, she continued to move down and got to the wet pussy. She caressed her clitoris, swollen with excitement, with her tongue and fingered her vagina, which was flowing with juice. Victoria moaned in pleasure. Then Diana, to add fuel to the fire, accelerated her movements with her fingers, and Vika howled from overexcitation like a police siren!

Chapter 7

Diana woke up in the same locker room, her body ached from lashes. Like a leper, she was covered in scratches and abrasions. My throat was dry and I was terribly thirsty. Finding no liquid in the dressing room, Diana cautiously tiptoed down the corridor to the kitchen. Suddenly, something unexpectedly rustled under her feet, Diana shuddered and saw a rat. Shrieking with all her might, Diana stamped her feet and began to cry. The rat also turned out to be shy, waving its tail goodbye, the frightened rat disappeared into the darkness. Suddenly, a light came on at the end of the corridor and Diana, like a moth, headed for a bright glow. Entering the chic hall, from where a bright radiance emanated, Diana saw a table covered with decorations. There were lighted candles on the table, a couple of glasses, silver cutlery, a bottle of expensive champagne lay in a stainless steel ice bucket. The food on the table was luxurious and testified to the rich life of the owner. A heavy plate of grainy red caviar tartlets, truffles, lobster, biscuit pudding, strawberries and a huge basket of ripe peaches. Hungry Diana, like a ferocious predator, pounced on the culinary splendor and devoured delicacies in a chaotic manner, munching on biscuit pudding with strawberries, lobsters and tartlets.

Bon Appetit. Pornographer said.

Thank you. Diana muttered with her mouth full.

Are you okay? You slept for almost two days...

Seriously? Diana swallowed the last piece of pudding. For two whole days?

Don't worry, it won't affect your payment in any way. We will assume that this is the cost of production.

Diana again remembered her sick mother.

May I call you? she asked.

Certainly. The pornographer handed her a cell phone.

Sure that her mother's health had improved, Diana found out one more detail: someone had hired a nurse for her bedridden mother. She looked suspiciously at the Pornographer, asking him with a look: "Did you do it?". The pornographer nodded in the affirmative.

Tell Mom I'll be back in ten days! Joyful Diana said goodbye and hung up.

Then Diana took a banana from the table and, pretending that it was a penis, began to depict the act of oral sex. She drove a yellow banana between her breasts, licked it and sucked it. She took a banana in her mouth and caressed her wet pussy with her fingers. Ripping off the banana skin with her teeth, Diana did not notice how the Pornographer approached her, took the banana from her and threw it aside. Seeing a sad face, he took out his cock from his pants and put a red-hot rod in her mouth. Grasping the head with her lips, Diana began to work with her mouth to deliver true pleasure to her master. Swallowing a member as deeply as possible, Diana choked a little on a part of the male flesh, but soon got a taste, and she even began to like to play on the verge of subtle pleasure and debauchery. Diana accelerated the movements of her mouth ... Feeling that the ejaculation was close, she madly wanted the Pornographer to cum on her face! However, Pornographer closed his eyes and stood motionless. Then Diana took the cock in her hands and pulled it hard until the Pornographer splashed a volley of sticky webs on her lips. Feeling the pleasant taste of sperm, Diana licked her lips appetizingly, took a red strawberry from the table and put it in her mouth, smiling pleasantly.

After an amazing suction, Diana pulls the tablecloth off the table along with the remnants of food, and wrapping herself in the tablecloth as if in a blanket, she fell asleep soundly. Diana woke up in the morning. She was awakened by some voices and loud noises coming from the street. Listening more carefully, Diana realized that these were the screams of guest workers who were unloading a truck with building materials. Wrapped up better in a tablecloth, Diana noticed a cleaner who silently washed the floors and did not pay any attention to Diana.

I'm sorry… Diana said. Where can you get cold water here?

The cleaning lady looked away from the floor and stared at Diana with a smile and asked:

You our boss fuck? Yes?

What?! Diana was outraged.

Fuck ... He you cancer? The cleaning lady paraphrased her question with an Uzbek accent.

To some extent, yes. Timidly confirmed Diana.

Water in the kitchen, it's straight and to the right. The cleaner said, satisfied with the answer.

In the kitchen, Diana made coffee and made a cheese sandwich. Having managed to take just one sip of a fragrant invigorating drink, all the solitude was broken by the cleaning lady who entered the kitchen, who again asked:

Does the boss have a big dick? Does he fuck you?

Diana choked at such a tactless question, soiling her robe out white tablecloth...

Fuck, fuck! So that sparks fly from the eyes! Diana snarled angrily.

Oh ... The cleaning lady was taken aback, rounding her narrow Asian eyes in surprise.

Better tell me, where is the shower, far away? Diana asked.

You have a shower in the locker room. Didn't you know? Have you been fucked there yet?

Indeed, there was a shower in the locker room, and a locker in the shower. Diana found a familiar ointment in it, with which Vika smeared abrasions from a lash. On another shelf were lubricants for anal sex. Diana opened one bottle, the rich smell of strawberries hit her nostrils sharply. The strawberry smell of debauchery was intoxicating and exciting. In order not to be tempted again, Diana closed the bottle, and with it the cabinet.

After taking a relaxing shower, Diana discovered new collections of underwear in the dressing room. Trying on the first model that came across, Diana looked at herself in the mirror. Soft silk underwear with exquisite lace embodies the epitome of beauty and elegance. Any ugly fool, wearing such underwear, will turn on any male from a half turn and receive from him at least more than one night of hot love. Any man who sees a woman in this lingerie is doomed to an erection feeling a hard stiff cock in his pants. Beautiful underwear helps better than any Viagra. Suddenly, Diana saw a bloody medical gown in the corner, taking the gown in her hands, she noticed a badge on it with the inscription: Angela. "Where is he from?" thought Diana. All this is very strange ... There is obviously dried blood on the dressing gown. Who is this Angela? What if they killed her?!

Diana froze for a second, making a disappointing conclusion: “What if they kill me too ?! They will slaughter like a pig in one take! They will release the guts, and then they will say, this is your role, you are our victim. It's all suspicious and strange... Really, why was she lured here at all? What is this Pornographer up to?! Loud steps began to be heard from the corridor, Diana wanted to scream, but could not make a sound.

Chapter 8. Flashbacks

The footsteps intensified, Diana opened the door and saw before her the Pornographer in the form of the Joker.

Put on your medical gown and follow me. He said dryly.

Numb with shock, Diana nodded her head obediently, complied with the request of the Pornographer and followed him down the dark corridor. She had never been in this room before, even though it wasn't a room at all. Brick walls, chains hanging from the ceiling, water dripping from somewhere in the corner.

Get up against the wall. The pornographer commanded.

What are you? Diana asked fearfully. Are you going to shoot me here?

Stand against the wall and take off your robe. Viciously repeated the Pornographer. Otherwise I'll feed you to the rats...

Where? Here? So okay?

Fine. Put your hands up

Listen, what kind of strange fantasies do you have. Of course, I understand that in life I want to try everything, but this is already too much ...

The pornographer snapped iron shackles around her wrists.

I would clap your hands, it's a pity your hands are busy. Diana snapped.

But the Pornographer had no time for jokes, he took out a knife and approached Diana ... The pornographer ran the tip of the knife over her body as if drawing patterns. Diana closed her eyes tightly. He will still kill me! He will slaughter ... And remember your name. The cold blade touched her body again, another second and the cold steel would enter her flesh. The pornographer waved his hand lightly, skillfully cut the straps of her bra, leaving Diana in only lace panties. She stood bare-chested and her eyes wide open with excitement. The pornographer carefully ran the blade along the silk fabric to the left and right, Diana's panties fell to her feet. Smooth-shaven pussy beckoned to her, exciting and not without that swollen member of the Pornographer. He threw the knife aside, took off his pants, and entered Diana.

Oh how good! Diana, hanging on chains, screamed.

The pornographer accelerated his movements and fucked defenseless Diana like a devil. The iron pins that held the shackles were shaking. Dusty sand fell from the ceiling. Diana continued to moan. Raindrops pounded on the roof. The pornographer fucked Diana to the beat of the hitting drops. Thunder struck hard, deafening the entire space of the torture chamber. The pornographer came into Diana and her pussy felt sticky warm cum that slowly dripped down her thighs. The pornographer picked up a medical gown, wiped the remnants of sperm from his penis with it and threw a crumpled rag at Diana's feet. Without saying a word, he left the room. Fucked to convulsions, Diana hung senselessly on the chains. The pins could not stand it and broke away from the ceiling. Clattering with her shackles, Diana fell to the concrete floor. Having broken her knees in the blood, she lay unconscious, entangled in iron fetters.

***

Diana woke up again in her dressing room, her wounded knees were treated with iodine and brilliant green. Her hands ached from the heavy chains... She reluctantly got up from the couch and heard some noise. Leaving the door of the dressing room, Diana realized that this was a man's cry. Following the noise, she entered the hall, where the Pornographer was sitting on the floor with a bottle of whiskey and crying.

Do you know why whiskey has such square bottles?

No… Diana shook her head.

So that she never rolls away from her master. The pornographer answered. It's a pity other things don't have this option...

For instance? Diana asked.

For example, when choosing your life path.

This is what I have had since childhood. When I was a teenager, I watched through a hole in the wall as my mother had sex with other men. I began to make sketches of these orgies and then sold the drawings to classmates. Once, one of the teachers caught me selling erotic pictures and called my mother to school. As a result, I was sent to a psychiatric hospital. Having imitated recovery and safely discharged, after graduating from school I entered VGIK at the directing department. What a mistake it was! Classic movie, who needs it?! I have always liked commercials and erotic scenes from several films more ... For example, in the movie "9th Company" there is an episode where young recruits together fuck a girl named Snow White. One even confesses his love to her and, to universal applause, calls her: “The Sea Goddess Cyprida.” Or in the film "DMB", the hero, nicknamed the Bayonet, has a widow with cancer in a crypt, not far from the grave of her deceased husband. The whole world is built on nine seconds of orgasm. But this is all poetry, the prose of life is much harsher. I was expelled from VGIK in my last year, they did not allow me to defend my graduation film. In their opinion, I shot too explicit a movie. I did not begin to recover, got a job in an advertising company, filmed all sorts of videos and other advertisements for sex shops. And then he opened his own porn studio.

Chapter 9

The drunken Pornographer sipped some more whiskey and started crying again. He sobbed like an offended boy whose parents did not buy another toy. Diana felt sorry for him.

Her! Well, what are you! Stop it ... She consoled the Pornographer.

But the Pornographer roared even harder, sniffing, plentiful men flowing down his unshaven cheeks.

Oh, stop it. Diana tried to hug him, but the Pornographer capriciously rejected her hugs. Stop crying, I say ... You are so cool! A real man. Nobody fucked me like that! You fucked me like a real male, put me in my place.

Truth? The pornographer stopped crying and cheered up a little.

Of course it's true! We women, in fact, only this is what we need! To put cancer and wound hair around a fist ...

Forgive me. The drunken pornographer began to justify himself. You're so good…

This passion for eroticism did not appear immediately. It's all mother, bitch! If she didn’t take men home, wouldn’t give them all in a row right and left ... Perhaps this would not have happened ... You might even have seen her.

Come on? Diana was surprised. When is this?

Do you remember when we met for the first time in a bar and you gave me a blowjob in the toilet. My mother works there as a cleaner. Thought you might have seen her, such a lean old woman with evil eyes.

No, I don't remember anything. Diana lied, and the phrase immediately sounded in her head: “Well, get out of here you slut under the fence!”. Withering with evil eyes, you say? No, I didn't see it for sure.

Diana felt even more sorry for him. Poor man, he is not to blame for anything, in childhood, a crazy mother broke his whole psyche. She stroked the Pornographer's cheek and kissed him. Diana felt dizzy, but the Pornographer held her back, not letting her fall. They collapsed on a small sofa next to them and merged into a warm embrace. The pornographer shoved his hands under her blouse and felt for the lack of a bra, passionately squeezing her swollen nipples. Diana's words, that he is real and fucks her best of all, motivated her to new exploits. Diana unzipped his fly and put her hand in his shorts. But the time in the pants of the Pornographer showed half past five. Feeling the confusion on the part of his partner, Pornographer seized the initiative and penetrated like a nimble snake into her panties. Gently and gently fingering her clitoris. A pleasant shiver ran through Diana's body, she closed her eyes and enjoyed the sweet fingers that entered her. She even tried to excite the Pornographer one more time, but his flaccid cock did not want to turn into a hard stone bayonet. Their joint petting was interrupted by a phone call. The pornographer took out his phone from the back pocket of his jeans. Turns out it was the producer. Director Serebrov was given a suspended sentence today, so a new project is soon planned, where the Pornographer's film studio can be involved. We decided to discuss the details at the upcoming porn conference in Berlin. After finishing the conversation, Pornographer took another sip of whiskey, put his head on the pillow and began to snore. The bottle slipped from his weakened hand, hit the floor, but did not break. “They know how to do it! Diana thought. Not like our vodka, any fall and smithereens. The difference between vodka and whiskey is the same as the difference between sexual partners. Whiskey is more expensive than vodka, therefore, a person who consumes whiskey is financially more prosperous. Although this does not insure against idle misfires ... Diana looked with tenderness at the snoring Pornographer and made a disappointing conclusion that alcohol has a detrimental effect on potency and it does not matter how much it costs. There was another phone call. This time, the screeching sound came from far away. Listening carefully, Diana realized that the call was coming from the Pornographer's office. “Hmm, very strange. Diana caught herself thinking. He usually always locks his office." Moving to the sound of a ringing phone, Diana was solving the dilemma of answering or not answering the call? There is no prohibition on using a home phone in the contract. So why not pick up the phone? Especially later, after the end of the conversation, you can call your mother. I wonder how she is? Diana entered the office, went to the table, looked at the receiver for a few seconds and the call stopped. Slightly taken aback by this turn of events, Diana looked at the phone in confusion.

Who did not have time, he was late. Diana said and the phone rang again.

This time, Diana resolutely grabbed the phone and said: "Hello."

This is a police investigator. It came from the other end of the tube.

Yes, I'm listening to you. Diana's voice trembled.

Your employee Angela Snezhina was found dead today.

Where did you find it?

In a ditch near Moscow, not far from the fish farm. Someone slit her throat, and then undressed to the goal ... So she lay naked, until one dog breeder accidentally discovered.

Cut your throat? Diana whispered.

Her relatives told us that she worked at your film studio, as an actress or something ... Are you a secretary? We can meet with you, need to clarify the details?

Yes, I'm a secretary. Diana lied, and she thought: “If you really knew who I work here ...”.

So can we meet? The investigator repeated his question.

Yes. Diana chimed in. Where should you go for interrogation?

What are you, what an interrogation. The investigator laughed. A formal conversation, you need to clarify the personal connections of the murdered and other details.

I can only in a week. I remembered about the contract Diana.

Let's do it, I'll look at the studio myself in a few days ... Agreed?

Agreed ... Diana hung up the phone, sweat beaded on her forehead.

It seems that this is the same Angela, Diana found her badge on a bloody medical gown. Now it is clear what kind of shooting! First they fuck you until you lose your pulse, and then they cut you until you lose consciousness. Black market porn, dirty dismemberment... And Diana is just a pathetic pawn in this cannibalistic game.

Diana! Where are you going bitch?! Aggressively shouted the awakened Pornographer.

He furiously searched for his slave, his terrible voice came closer and closer. Diana, in a panic, was looking for a place to hide from the executioner, but the Pornographer's office was arranged in such a way that it did not have any cabinets or secret hiding places. Then Diana just crawled under the table and sobbing nervously began to wait for her death. Suddenly, under the table, she found a crumpled piece of paper. Unfolding and smoothing the crumpled sheet, Diana saw a photograph of a naked red-haired girl. The image of a girl is crossed out with a cross. On the reverse side was the signature: Angela Snezhina.

What the hell are you doing in my office?! The Pornographer, leaning under the table, asked angrily.

Chapter 10

I just got scared. Diana spoke up.

What?! Scared?! The pornographer did not believe.

Diana crawled out from under the table, Pornographer took a step towards her. In order to somehow protect herself, Diana blurted out: "The investigator called. He said that Angela was killed! He will be here shortly for a formal talk." The pornographer stepped back. The news of Diana's death frightened him... a little, Pornographer flared up.

Angela was killed, you say ... What the hell?!

How do I know? I did kill her.

Angela bitch. We have a shoot scheduled for tomorrow. Plus he owes me a lot of money.

Was she also your slave? And starred in your dirty films under the same contract?

Shut up! Not your body!

I understand… Diana covered her mouth with her hand for a moment. It was you who killed her.

The pornographer takes Diana by the hand and tries to take her out from your office. Diana breaks free and tries to run away from him.

***

They were separated only by a

desk. Diana on one side, Pornographer on the other. Diana with a jerk threw off the monitor and folders with documents from the table, she wanted to disorient Pornographer and rushed to the left. But Pornographer figured out her plan, grabbed her by the hair and dragged her into the locker room. He locked Diana in the dressing room and, judging by the strong hitting the main entrance door left the film studio. The door to the dressing room was also not made of plywood, and no matter how much Diana knocked on it with her hands and feet, the steel rectangular structure remained impregnable. in desperation Diana began to cry, gradually tears changed to hysteria. “God, why did I agree to this shooting?! She roared. What if he went away for a week and left her here to starve? No, he is still a great original and came up with a more interesting death for her. To starve me to death is too petty for him."

Finding in a pile of things a shirt that was three sizes too big for Diana, she wrapped herself in it like a dressing gown and fell asleep. She dreamed of memories from childhood, how she sits on her mother's lap, beloved mother reads a book to her. Diana drinks hot milk with honey, her mother gently strokes her hair, then hugs her tightly and says: "Even if everything is bad now, then everything will always be fine later." The door to the room suddenly opens and the Pornographer appears. Diana turns her head, her mother is nowhere to be found.

Stop spinning, bitch! commanded The pornographer gave Diana a slap in the face.

He then grabbed the helpless Diana by the hair and dragged her into the bath. He thrust Diana's head under the stream of cold water, resisting

Diana rested her hands on the sink. Then the Pornographer pulled off her jeans along with her panties and inserted her hot cock into her vagina. His testicles beat against Diana's buttocks, he squeezed her breasts and said: "My bitch ... Only mine." At the moment of ejaculation, he stroked her pubis so that he felt his sperm with his fingertips. Diana moaned from the pleasant pain, but at the same time she hated the Pornographer for allowing himself to treat her like that. He shoved his cum-smeared fingers into her mouth, forcing her to lick them. It cannot be said that Diana was disgusted, but she did not receive much pleasure either. But having received another slap from the Pornographer, she immediately pretended that she had dreamed of such a dessert all her life.

The Pornographer's phone rang. Answering the call and saying: "I'll be there soon." He turned to Diana.

to me Now I need to take a break. You can rest for now.

After everything I've been through… I don't need to rest, it's time for me to retire! Diana snapped.

In general, relax. The pornographer smiled. Here's your phone, you can even call your mother. I warn you right away, you can only call the hospital. Calls to other numbers are blocked.

Who would doubt that. Diana noted.

Oh yes! I almost forgot. Pornographer said. You will receive SMS on this phone, so be in touch. This is included in the terms of the contract.

Chapter 11

Indeed, Pornographer did not deceive. The next night, Diana woke up from a text message signal. She thought it was an alert from the hospital. New information about mother's health has appeared. Therefore, she jumped up so abruptly and fixed her eyes on the text of the incoming message. Unfortunately, it was completely different. Diana put the phone aside. The pain in my cheekbones from the blows made it impossible to concentrate. It is not clear, was it all in a dream or in reality? Recently received SMS required a response. Diana took the phone in her hands and entered into correspondence.

PORNOGRAPH. Personally, my penis is now like a wooden one.

DIANA. Tell me how hard is he?

PORNOGRAPH. I'm very excited right now. My sinewy cock is very hard. I need to de-stress, do you agree?

DIANA. I insert my fingers into my hole between my legs. And I feel so good ... Unbearably good that you feel me exactly ... From the fact that you know that I'm doing this right now I'm thinking about you, about the inevitability of the approaching finish line. I really want to take it in your mouth! I just can't think about it.

PORNOGRAPH. Oh yeah. Write how you caress my penis?

DIANA. My tongue slides over him, up and down. I bite it a little and stroke it with two fingers. Licking, kissing and...

PORNOGRAPH. Do you swallow or is it better for you to cum on your chest?

DIANA. Do everything to the end, and do not leave me. I want to know your taste, the taste of your sperm, your body ... Feel how your fingers spread my flesh, I want to feel pain, and so that you do not hold back with me, but do what you want for real!

PORNOGRAPH. Uu... I'm ready

to kiss you in the stomach and down, down, down... Come on, lie down, I'll lick your pussy and pull it with my fingers.

DIANA. I agree. And I'm still bleeding, wet and hot, sticky, trembling... Tired, ready to lose consciousness, to fall beyond the bounds of the permissible, together with you.

PORNOGRAPH. Is your pussy shaved?

DIANA. Absolutely smooth (naked). Put your fingers in me, tongue?

PORNOGRAPH. Yes... Are you okay? Do you still want me?

DIANA. I experienced several short strong orgasms almost in a row, and the desire did not go away ... It feels like if you touch me, I will bite my lips again and again ... Very strong sensations! The constant feeling that another second, and I will finish ...

And I want you to enter into me strongly and to the end. Please do this to me!

PORNOGRAPH. I keep moving... Touch your wet pussy, and enter it with your fingers, feel me! I now took a member in my hand and pull it, I feel good.

DIANA. Touch your dick, close your eyes, I'm with you. Just believe. I am yours tonight. I slow down when I write, then again I start stroking, sliding, pinching, pressing the clitoris, but my fingers do not obey and slip into the vagina, squeeze through the hot flesh, press against the walls and to the G-spot. And in these moments, I stop writing to you ... I freeze, close my eyes and imagine how I lick you everywhere, take your dick in my mouth, wrap my lips around it, you insert it deep, so deep that it’s hard to breathe ... You are not in a hurry, you are looking at me, then you take your dick out of my mouth and enter me from behind. You slowly introduce it into me, gradually to the end ... You make several movements and cum inside me, continuing to move ...

PORNOGRAPH. I want to cum in your mouth!

DIANA. Okay. Only first I will wrap my lips around your cock ... We both will cease to exist at this moment, we will merge into a single whole, we will mix ...

PORNOGRAPH. I'll finish soon. Are you swallowing?

DIANA. Hold a little, I'll swallow a little.

PORNOGRAPH. I'm holding. Tell me when you're ready.

DIANA. Get started!

PORNOGRAPH. I'm cumming!

DIANA. Come on, come on! Delicious…

PORNOGRAPH. Uff … Wow! Mmmmm...

DIANA. I swallowed everything down to the last drop.

PORNOGRAPH. Have you finished?

DIANA. It does not matter. I feel good from your desire ... From the thought that we did it. All shut up. Satisfied and exhausted ... With a clitoris hard as a bud ... The vagina is hot, hot. I will break and come very soon, very soon.

PORNOGRAPH. I'm off.

DIANA. Awesome feelings! It's unbelievable how good I feel!

Chapter 12

Waking up, Diana found that the phone had disappeared. But instead, bottles of mineral water and several boxes of pizza appeared on the table. There was a note on the boxes: “Sit here and don't stick your head out! It's better for your safety...Your

Pornographer." Diana tugged at the doorknob, the door was still closed.

Do you think I have a choice? She said irritably, not yet knowing that she would have to be locked up for the next few days.

A few days later, the door lock finally clicked, notifying the captive that the exit from the dressing room was open. A little confused and not completely believing that the door is still open. Diana cautiously left the dressing room, but the corridor was empty. Having experienced a fit of yeast, she walked cautiously into the main hall, hoping to see the Pornographer there. But there was no one in the hall either.

Hey! A voice called out.

Turning around, Diana saw a girl in a strict black suit. The girl's face looked familiar. She had seen him somewhere before. Exactly! I think her name is Victoria? Only then Victoria was in a red tight dress. It was Vika who smeared Dina's body with a cream for abrasions. And then there was the stunning sex...

Are you alone here? Victoria asked suspiciously.

Seems to be yes…

Have you heard of Angela?

Diana nodded silently.

Nightmare! Victoria was frightened. A girl was stabbed to death in broad daylight. Knife to the throat and thrown into a ditch!

Yes, I know the investigator called me.

Investigator?

Yes, police investigator. He even promised to visit here.

Come over here? What for?

He said to clarify some formalities.

Oh, those formalities. Victoria grinned wickedly. One fiction only. It hurts him to mess around with the murder of some porn actress.

You think?

Certainly! It's just for show that he works out working hours. And the killer has not been found.

It's always like this in our country...

And what am I talking about! They will hesitate, murmur, and put the matter on the brakes.

Are you filming here too? Diane turned the conversation in a different direction.

Of course not! What are you? Victoria was surprised. I work here as a lawyer.

I’m sorry, I didn’t mean to offend you at all ... It’s just ... Well, you remember that time ... So I thought that you ...

Ah, you're talking about it! Yes, I have such a character trait! I can’t help myself… You don’t have to apologize, it’s all right. I really used to work here as a porn actress. It was a long time ago when Pornographer just opened his first studio.

Wow…

Yes! After shooting like this for several years, I realized that I wanted something different. I'm fed up with all these penises and other genitals ... I went to study to be a lawyer, count up? Entered Moscow State University.

At MSU?

Why, just pay money and a diploma in your pocket. Studied on a paid basis. A doctor of jurisprudence wrote a diploma for me. Of course, I had to suck him off later, he was a terrible pervert, he quoted everything from Homer ... But let's not talk about sad things.

Wow.

Yes, this is my career path. They just didn't hire me...

Even with a diploma from Moscow State University?! Diana was surprised.

Imagine, they didn’t call back from a single interview! Freaks! Victoria considered. It was only later that I realized that the main thing is not a diploma, but what is in your head.

As they say, learn from mistakes? And a negative experience, is that also a kind of experience?

Here, here! That's what I'm talking about! As a result, she again went to work for the Pornographer, but only as a graduate. Victoria laughed. A lawyer with a diploma, so to speak ... But you know, sometimes it’s so tempting to have sex on camera, even as a wolf howl! I can't help myself! You yourself are not yet addicted to this drug of debauchery?

It seems not ... So far I do not feel such symptoms in myself.

Diana and Victoria fell silent. The hall immediately became quiet, only the fan blades whirled under the ceiling with a slight creak. Victoria looked around the space angrily, then exclaimed.

Listen! Are you tired of sitting here?

Not the right word ... As in a hot frying pan.

I was just thinking, what's the point of having a steam bath here? Because of this murder, the Pornographer will still be gone for a few days. Shall we go for a ride out of town? It will be great!

I don’t even know ... Diana doubted. It may be against my contract.

So you don't even have to worry about it. I bet no one will miss you here. Besides, the Pornographer is a normal person and won't get angry if you're away for just a few hours.

Oh… I don’t even know… I’d better go to the hospital to see my mother if I can be away for a few hours.

Listen, where I call you ... Victoria made a significant pause. There will be one very cool doctor. And he just specializes in strokes.

Truth?

Of course it's true! He is the best professional! World class doctor! He will advise you, tell you what medicines to buy, which clinic is better to go to.

It seems that they have already hired a nurse for my mother and it seems that the situation is getting better.

It 's one thing to be a nurse, and another thing to be a professional doctor! There may not be a second such possibility.

Why so?

He flies back to Israel tomorrow and it is not known when he will be back in Russia. I thought the health of your own mother is really dear to you, but it turns out you don’t care ...

No, it's not like that at all. For me, this is really very important ... It’s just that something is a little noisy in my head, so I can’t figure it out right away. Of course, I agree to go to your party. Diana smiled.

Well, it's not quite a party… Victoria hesitated. So it's more just a friendly meeting ... But you made the right decision. In any case, it will be much better than being cooped up in that stinking hangar.

Diana remembered the last days spent locked up in the dressing room, and flared up.

Really, what's the point of sitting here?! Waiting for a jade rod of love to be shoved up your ass?! I've had enough of these feelings! I need to pause and meet with the doctor, perhaps in the near future my mother will need treatment abroad.

***

The car turned sharply to the side and moved off the asphalt road onto the dirt road. It got a little dark.

You said we were going to a party, didn't you? Diana got nervous.

Well, yes. It will be such a country party ... By the way, we have almost arrived.

Stop the car! I have changed my mind! Diana screamed in panic, clutching the steering wheel.

Calm down. Victoria sharply pressed the gas pedal and increased her speed. Don't stop me from driving, or we'll crash.

Loosening her grip, Diana let go of the steering wheel and tried to open the door at full speed in order to jump out of the passenger compartment. But all attempts were in vain, the doors were tightly blocked.

I tell you again, calm down. Victoria slowed down. The pornographer wants to kill you, you know?

Diana froze with horror pondering the meaning of the words spoken.

How to kill? Me?

Yes! I couldn't tell you before. There's a studio in the hangar full of cameras, everything is recorded. I thought we'd come to the place, and I'll tell you everything in a calm atmosphere. And you see, you start freaking out! Grab the wheel...

Sorry. I thought…

She thought… Victoria snapped offendedly. You'd better think about where that bloody robe with the badge came from?

Diana shrugged.

That's it ... And you need to move your brains and better understand people! Pornographer, he's a real psycho! Maniac! A man without principles will sell his own mother for money.

Diana remembered the cleaner from the bar and mentally agreed with Victoria.

He removes dismemberment for private customers. And he wanted to use you as another victim

It can't be… Diana whispered.

Maybe ... How else can! Consider that you are very lucky, otherwise you would be filming tonight in his next dungeon, where you would be slaughtered like a stupid sheep in the spotlight.

At that moment, Diana saw a huge sign: “FISH FARM. OUTSIDE ENTRANCE IS FORBIDDEN!!!”. Bouncing on the bumps, the car drove a few more kilometers. Victoria looked around with concern and parked the car near the ravine.

Come out… She hissed at Diana.

Victoria pulled a knife from the

glove compartment.

I'd love to get out of here, but the doors are locked.

Already unlocked. If you don't come out in a second, I'll cut you right here.

Deciding not to stain the velvet upholstery with blood. Diana unquestioningly left the car and even tried to run away, but tripped over a snag and fell into the mud. Helplessly floundering in a huge puddle of mud, she soon saw Victoria in front of her. Another second and this specialist with a diploma from Moscow State University will slash Diana's throat with a knife, releasing a blood-red fountain from the carotid artery. Diana closed her eyes, according to all the laws of logic, death was inevitable.

Chapter 13

Diana found a stone under her

hand. Grabbing the life-saving weapon, she hit the lawyer on the head with it. Stunned, Victoria squinted her eyes, dropped the knife from her hand, and slumped to the ground.

Sterlet, painted! Diana blurted out.

Lying unconscious, Victoria kept an icy silence. Groaning and stumbling, Diana somehow hobbled to the roadway. But passing cars drove by indifferently, apparently their drivers did not want to have anything to do with the grubby creature from the side of the road, which actively waved its arms, urging them to stop and give a lift to a hitherto unknown creation of nature.

The rescue has finally arrived! The old Zhiguli stopped at the unfortunate martyr. A toothless grandfather looked out of the window of a rusty carriage.

With a cunning squint, he began to examine the extraordinary miracle Yudo.

Delighted, Diana ran up to the car, pulled the handle, but the door was closed. The toothless grandfather took out an iPhone from somewhere in his armpit and photographed an outlandish beast. Diana was furious at what was happening. Having crossed himself, the grandfather started his old jalopy and, smoking the transparent sky with black exhausts, drove off into the distance, only shouting goodbye: “Go to yourselves in peace, bigfoot!”.

What?! Big Foot?! So no one has insulted me yet! Diana was outraged.

Another car with tinted windows pulled up beside her.

Ah, here comes another pervert. Do you want sex with a Bigfoot?

The tinted window rolled down and Diana saw the Pornographer in front of her.

Now is not the time for jokes. Get in the car immediately! He commanded.

Diana obeyed implicitly and sat in the back seat. Feeling safe in the car, Diana fell asleep.

***

Opening her eyes, Diana looked around wearily. She was still in the same dressing room in the Pornographer's lair.

It can't be! She exclaimed. Did I dream it all? And none of this happened?

Diana tried to remember how events unfolded, but her headache prevented her. After taking a cold shower, small fragments of memories gradually began to emerge in my memory ... After the Pornographer picked her up on the highway, they spent the night in some roadside hotel. He pushed Diana onto the bed and slowly removed her panties. He unbuttoned her bra and began to gently caress her breasts. He went down lower and lower ... His tongue slipped into the vagina. Diana felt hot and humid. The pornographer tickled her clitoris with his tongue and she felt divinely good. After licking her smooth pussy, Pornographer used his hands. He made a homemade gag out of a sheet and stuffed Diane's mouth with it. He rubbed her clit with his fingers so that Diana howled loudly and moaned with pleasure. At that moment, the bed beneath them collapsed! The pornographer grabbed a chair that fell under his arm and broke the window with it. He swept away the fragments with the help of a pillow and led Diana to the windowsill. Diana put a pillow under her chest and leaned on it, standing with her back to the Pornographer. He lightly lubricated her anus and inserted his hot cock into her narrow passage. Diana groaned, the broken window no longer holding back the sounds. The pornographer fucked Diana hard and brutally. He tore her like a stray cat to a street cat during estrus. And in this animal copulation, all the burning passion of the past night was laid.

No, she couldn't have imagined it. Diana spoke out loud. Such sex does not happen in dreams, only in reality!

Three days remained until the end

of the contract. After all that Diana has been forced to endure, she decides to renegotiate the terms of the contract. “I didn’t sign up for this, and this crazy Vika with a knife in her hand! I do not need such happiness! The pornographer must pay me for moral damages. We need to revise the terms of the contract immediately!

***

The film set was empty.

Hey! Is there anyone? She called out.

There was no answer. Only the rustling wind howled unpleasantly in the silence, emphasizing Diana's loneliness in the empty room. The door to the Pornographer's office was locked. Then Diana grabbed a nearby chair and slammed it with all her might on the doorknob.

So, just a little bit more... The burglar Diana groaned. And one more time! One, two... Got it!

As a result, after a series of strong blows, the lock broke and the door successfully opened. It was from this office that she learned about the corpse of Angela Snezhina. Turning her head to the right, Diana saw a closed safe. A massive iron box with a combination lock stood as an impregnable fortress. Hacking such a contraption will take a lot of time and it’s not a fact that Diana will be able to pick up an encoded cipher at all! But she was lucky, all the necessary documents were on the table. In addition to the signed contract she needed, there were also no less curious papers on the table. One red folder caught her eye.

Having opened it and carefully read the information contained there, Diana learns that everything that happens around is a vile and dirty game of the Pornographer. A low-end subscription reality show for one of the streaming platforms.

Pornographer, motherfucker! I believed you! Diana screamed.

She sat down at the computer, went to her bank account and transferred the money received from the Pornographer to another account. Half the job is already done. Then Diana picked up the landline phone from the table and called the clinic where her terminally ill mother was. At first no one answered, but she still got through.

Hello! Yes, prepare the operation, I have money. Now I'm 100% sure...

Suddenly, during a telephone conversation, Diana sees through the window how the Pornographer's car drove up to the entrance to the filming pavilions. The driver carefully parked, the door opened and a man in a black mask stepped out of the car. The masked man looked around and entered the building.

Chapter 14

The door screeched open and the Pornographer entered the office. He took off his mask and yelled furiously at Diana, “What the hell are you doing here?! I told you to sit in the locker room and keep your head down!”

Do not shout at me! Diana snapped. I'm not your maid.

You are wrong, my dear. You are a maid. What a maid... According to the contract, for three days I can do whatever I want with you. Otherwise, I have the right to return my money back.

This money is no longer in your account. Diana interrupted.

What?!

According to the contract, we did not agree that I should participate in a reality show on a paid subscription.

What other show? Totally crazy? I don't know anything about any show... You better tell me why the hell did you crawl out of the locker room? You were told in Russian to sit there and not stick your head out! The pornographer tried to evade the answer and change the subject of the conversation.

I have long suspected that something is wrong here. Even when I came to my former boss, asking him to take me back to work. I accidentally noticed some kind of video broadcast from one of the employees in front of his office. I thought it was you and me in the video.

Interesting... And what did we do there? Did they just drink tea?

Don't clown. I signed the contract, and you brazenly smiled. Even then I thought that all this just seemed to me on a nervous basis. But then gradually the puzzles began to suddenly take shape in the big picture. Why was all this masquerade with dressing up necessary? All these strange images similar to the Joker and Harley Quinn?

The pornographer was thoughtfully silent.

You yourself remember. When I signed the contract, I asked you about the camera hanging in the corner above the ceiling. You once again lied to me, saying that this is a simple legal formality.

These are all your sick fantasies, you need to be treated. The pornographer chuckled.

And finally. Diana summed it up

firmly. I found this folder today. Does she have my fantasies too?

And in a rage she threw a red folder with documents in the face of the Pornographer. From contact with his physiognomy, the red folder opened and from it, like confetti from a firecracker, sheets scattered on the floor.

Hey, you definitely went off the rails! Throw it out again, you'll regret it.

I already regret contacting you. You bastard... Your own mother works as a cleaner in a bar, and you make millions and never helped her.

Thank God it's not live. The Pornographer breathed a sigh of relief. Otherwise, disgrace would not have been avoided. On the other hand, it's even good that you know everything. Otherwise, I kept thinking when the contract would end ... How can I explain all this to you later?

I know even more than you think.

Truth? And what else do you know?

I know that it was you who killed Angela Snezhina.

What?! Did I kill Angela? Are you out of your mind? The fact that Angela is still a creature and owes me money, I do not deny. But to take and kill a person, even that would not have crossed my mind. Besides, snuff porn is not my style.

Yeah of course. So I believed you, pervert.

He didn't really kill. An unfamiliar voice rang out.

The pornographer looked around fearfully.

I'm an investigator from the prosecutor's office. A stranger entered the office. I called you and warned you that I would come. Remember?

Diana nodded silently.

Apparently I was talking to you

then? Are you a secretary?

Somewhat. Answered instead of Diana Pornographer.

And you are apparently the director of this film studio Fedor Zyuzkin? Right? Just in case, the investigator clarified.

Hmm, he's the one. The Pornographer answered displeasedly, and thought to himself again: “Still, thank God that we are not on the air.”

Your boss didn't kill Angela Snezhina. The investigator turned to Diana. The fact is that your lawyer Victoria Glotova and your, let's say, former employee Angela were at the same time.

The interrogator hesitated for a moment, looked at the Pornographer and continued his accusatory story.

So, Victoria and Angela were laundering money behind your back. And then the received amounts were withdrawn through Western accounts to offshore companies. We are talking about several million dollars. The investigation established that Angela Snezhina was killed by her companion Victoria Glotova. We managed to get access to their correspondence. Snezhina began to blackmail Glotova, extorting money from her. She promised to tell everything to Pornographer if Glotova did not pay her a tidy sum. Their correspondence ends after an agreement to meet near the fish farm... She, in fact, had no choice. If the Pornographer would have found out about their black machinations, Glotova was threatened with a prison, a serious term. Therefore, Victoria decided to remove the blackmailer, simply slaughtered her like a stupid chicken, and threw the body into a ditch. Apparently she thought that they would not be able to find him there for a long time, but it turned out, on the contrary.

At that moment, a shot suddenly rang out in the office. The shot body of the investigator slammed to the floor, and a burgundy pool of blood spread around the murdered man.

Bravo! Bravo! Mr Investigator. Diana's sister Karina said as she entered the office.

Karina had a pistol in her hand.

Hey Pornographer! You see how easy it all turns out, and you were afraid. Karina continued. Oh little sister! Long time no see. Are you a star now? Videos with your participation on the first lines in the ratings of pornographic sites. There is progress! Talent! I remember your nude photo at school... By the way, it was also my idea to humiliate you in front of your classmates. A pornographer wouldn't have thought of that.

Diana cried.

Karin, that's enough. The

pornographer tried to stop the angry Karina.

Shut up! Karina cut him off sharply. Otherwise I'll put a bullet in your head!

The pornographer obediently fell silent.

I've always hated you Diana. Mother always loved you more! Of course, you are her favorite child from the best man in the world. And I'm an unexpected result of a drunken flight in a student hostel.

What are you carrying? Diana asked, crying.

One former classmate of our mother told me an interesting story. How this whore at the New Year's party was fucked in all the cracks by half the guys in the hostel.

It is not true! Diana screamed.

Wrong, it's true. She was fucked by three people at the same time! Then they cynically called this gang rape:

"Hockey triples of players and one goalkeeper" ... And nine months later I was born. Or did you forget, sister, that my birthday is in September, and our mother gave birth to me in the last year of the institute?

Arguing here was difficult, Diana continued to sob.

I have always hated you, little sister. We have been in a relationship with Pornographer since high school. This entire empire of the pornographic business belongs to me! The pornographer is just a pathetic six following my instructions. And when I found out that his sluts picked up from the street were laundering money behind my back, I decided to slam them both! I killed Angela, and then I persuaded Victoria to kill Diana by promising her a share of the Pornographer.

How is it my share? The pornographer was surprised.

This blowjob lawyer didn't even suspect that after the murder of Diana, I would hand her over to the cops with all the giblets... To be honest, I didn't expect Diana to be able to escape from Victoria. Also, I had no idea that the investigator from the prosecutor's office had access to their joint correspondence with Angela. Fortunately, no one guessed that I had come to the last meeting with Angela instead of Victoria. And it could turn out to be a misfire! But let's not talk about sad things ... I listened carefully to this "unfortunate detective" and, making sure that the investigation suspects Victoria of everything, I killed him. Karina casually kicked the investigator's bloodied corpse.

I don't understand just one thing. Diana sobbed. Why was this whole performance with the division of the apartment needed? If you have a million dollar fortune. Why do you need all this?

Silly Diana. I don't need this bugger for nothing. You still ask me about your alcoholic fiancé Ephraim, whom I bribed for three bottles of vodka to leave you. I wanted you and your mother to suffer. So that she suffers from pain in a hospital bed, and you, disgraced throughout the country, would rot in prison. But I see that you have already suffered enough, so I will ease your suffering and kill you. And the Pornographer will take all the blame and then tell the police that you tried to break the signed contract with him, transferred all the money to another account and even tried to kill him. And in self-defense, he had to shoot you.

Are there cameras around here? I will not do it. The frightened Pornographer got into the conversation.

I've turned off all my cameras.

Karina calmed him down. Either you kill her or I kill her. There is no third.

Covered with fear in a sticky sweat, Pornographer was frightenedly silent. His hands were trembling, and his heart was beating so hard that his chest was shaking.

Weakling! Karina strained through her teeth and shot at her sister.

The pornographer took a step forward and covered with his body the squinting Diana, who had already mentally prepared herself for death.

At that moment, someone's strong leg in a calf boot knocked out the window, and on the windowsill was a man in a black knitted mask and with a machine gun in his hands. The man was wearing a police uniform. He hit Karina on the head with the butt of a submachine gun, she dropped the pistol from her hand and fell unconscious. Following him, several more police officers appeared at the window. Two men in civilian clothes ran through the office door. Looking at the bloodied body of the Pornographer and the corpse of the investigator, one of them mournfully said: "We were late ...".

Chapter 15

An old bus rides along an old country road. Winter outside. All around are white expanses and a blizzard sweeps. Diana sat at the window and thought about something, looking into the snowy distance. Mom has already been discharged, she is now at home and is gradually on the mend, everything is fine with her. Mom does not know what happened to Karina, she thinks that her daughter just moved to live in another country, and for some reason she does not call or write to her anymore. In fact, Karina is in prison. For the murder of an employee in the line of duty, she was sentenced to the maximum possible term. Most likely, she will no longer be released, her full term of punishment will expire when she is already ninety-four years old!

Mom is sincerely grateful to her benefactor and, in spite of everything, believes that he is a very good person. Diana told her that he was in prison for the murder of lawyer Victoria Glotova. Mom doesn't know that the Pornographer took all the blame and wrote a frank confession to divert all suspicion from Diana. The court took into account the full confession and repentance of the defendant, imposing a sentence of fifteen years of general regime.

“Think! He hit me in the head with a stone, my mother said. Maybe this viper was the only way to stop it! Maybe she drank all the juice out of him! And he helped me like a god. If not for his money, I would be lying in the cemetery now. Hemorrhagic stroke, is it a joke?! Plus a heart complication and a heart attack to boot. Whoever says anything about him ... For me, he is a golden man, an angel-savior.

Diana was flooded with memories. Looking out the bus window, she also remembered when her mother was discharged from the hospital, they walked together through the winter city and they met the former fiancé Ephraim. He shivered from the cold and handed out flyers advertising "Fast Sushi Delivery" to all passers-by. Ephraim recognized Diana and her mother, and as if the naughty dog fawned over the owners: “Oh, hello! How are you mammy? Ephraim began his sycophantic monologue. And I work here... Take brochures, there will be a ten percent discount. Yes, we haven’t seen each other for a long time…" Diana looked at the former man indifferently.

Why are you silent like not relatives?! Ephraim asked, breathing fumes on his interlocutors.

Damn you! The mother hissed angrily.

You mama something again not in the spirit. Again, you are pouting about something. Let me hug you, mama.

Ephraim spread his arms, but in response received a spit in the face.

The traitor is gone. Shouted at the alcoholic mother.

Mom, leave him. Don't contact.

Why did I do this? Ephraim, stunned by this turn of events, asked.

How would Judas give you a nose! So that your eyes squint in a heap!

Don't get your hands dirty with this shit, better step over and move on. Diana calmed the heated mother.

And that's right! You will not wash

yourself off from this shushary later.

Moreover, you should not be nervous after the operation.

The daughter took her mother's arm and trampling the winter porridge from gray snow, they slowly trudged towards the metro. Behind him came the cries of the alcoholic Ephraim.

Sorry if that's not right. Anything can happen ... You will not be sorry for the drunken soul? Still, they were not strangers before.

***

The bus drove up to a fence with barbed wire.

We've arrived, the end! The bus driver said to the only passenger.

Dozing Diana opened her eyes and felt a terrible cold all around. The bus smelled of gasoline and tobacco smoke.

Come say! The driver repeated and looked at Diana appraisingly. Or have you changed your mind beautiful?! I know here one picturesque place ... Let's go and show you?

Diana looked at the driver suspiciously and thought about something.

Don't worry, I won't offend. Nobody has complained yet. Or do you need money? So this is not a problem, there is money, we will agree.

I don't need anything. Show your scenic spots to someone else. And it is better to spend money on a dentist, otherwise you don’t have half of your teeth. And those that remained, it’s scary to look at them, they are all rotten and brown. Moreover, I already have a beloved man and I will be faithful to him until the end of my life.

Diana walked along the fence, because of the bitter frost, she did not feel her fingers and toes. A strong wind was blowing and nasty snow was falling from the sky. She finally made it to the checkpoint. From there, she was sent to a long-term visitation facility, where a night was supposedly worth a suite in a five-star hotel in Dubai. Having somehow warmed up, Diana sat in painful thoughts ... A few hours later, the convoy brought the convict to the room.

He has changed a lot, turned gray and emaciated. His face reflected the mental anguish he had endured, which apparently still tormented him inwardly. Bags under the eyes indicated a lack of sleep. He was ashamed in front of Diana, he turned his eyes away and looked sullenly somewhere in the corner of the room. He felt guilty towards her. But he was glad to see her! Was glad she came! Here in prison, he thought a lot about her, often remembering her eyes and smile.

Hello beloved. She said.

He took a step towards her.

Stay where you are! The escort shouted.

The prisoner implicitly obeyed the command. The escort took a key from his pocket and unfastened the handcuffs, freeing his hands from the iron shackles.

So settle down here. The escort said in a softer tone. Kettle and microwave in the kitchen. Toilet and shower in the hallway. Do not go beyond these limits! It seems that he said everything, did not forget anything. I'll be back in three days around noon. Well, then I went.

As soon as the escort closed the door behind him. The pornographer felt an inexplicable excitement. He lifted his eyes and looked fixedly at Diana. She got out of bed and unbuttoned her down jacket and said: "I owe you three more days under the contract."

I don't have any more money. Produced by Pornographer.

He did not understand: "Why did she come here? After all, no one owes anything to anyone else!" The wound received from Karina's shot ached with new pain. He clutched his chest and coughed. Diana drew the curtains and took off her sweater. Then she went up to the Pornographer and, hugging his cheeks with her palms, kissed her beloved man on the lips.

It does not matter. She whispered. Whether you have money or not... I will still love you.

Her heart was beating harder and harder. His hands went down below Diana's breasts and unbuttoned her jeans, then he took off her panties. Time stood still and she felt him enter her.

www.ingramcontent.com/pod-product-compliance
Lightning Source LLC
LaVergne TN
LVHW010609160826
845677LV00013B/3321

* 9 7 9 8 4 0 8 6 8 2 0 1 0 *